RIP-ROARING RUSSELL

"Russell faces the challenges of growing up in his own inimitable way...being a big brother disturbs him because baby Elsa takes altogether too much of his mother's time, but by the book's end, he decides that it isn't so bad. Two, together, after all, can make much more noise."

—*School Library Journal*

Puffin Books by Johanna Hurwitz

Aldo Applesauce
Aldo Ice Cream
Much Ado About Aldo
The Rabbi's Girls
Rip-Roaring Russell
Russell Rides Again
Russell Sprouts

Johanna Hurwitz

Rip-Roaring RUSSELL

illustrated by Lillian Hoban

Puffin Books

PUFFIN BOOKS
Published by the Penguin Group
Viking Penguin Inc., 40 West 23rd Street, New York, New York 10010, U.S.A.
Penguin Books Ltd, 27 Wrights Lane, London W8 5TZ, England
Penguin Books Australia Ltd, Ringwood, Victoria, Australia
Penguin Books Canada Ltd, 2801 John Street, Markham, Ontario, Canada L3R 1B4
Penguin Books (N.Z.) Ltd, 182–190 Wairau Road, Auckland 10, New Zealand

Penguin Books Ltd, Registered Offices: Harmondsworth, Middlesex, England

First published in the United States of America by Greenwillow Books,
a division of William Morrow and Company, Inc. 1983.
Published in Puffin Books 1989 by arrangement with William Morrow and Company, Inc.

3 5 7 9 10 8 6 4 2

Text copyright © Johanna Hurwitz, 1983   Illustrations copyright © Lillian Hoban, 1983
All rights reserved

LIBRARY OF CONGRESS CATALOGING IN PUBLICATION DATA
Hurwitz, Johanna.   Rip-roaring Russell.
Reprint. Originally published: New York : Morrow, 1983.
Summary: Five-year-old Russell's adventures involve his nursery school,
his baby sister, and his friends in his apartment building.
[1. Nursery schools—Fiction. 2. Schools—Fiction. 3. Brothers and sisters —Fiction.
4. Apartment houses—Fiction] I. Hoban, Lillian, ill. II. Title.
PZ7.H9574Ri 1989 [Fic]   88–30683
ISBN 0-14-032939-0

Printed in the United States of America by R.R. Donnelley & Sons Company, Harrisonburg, VA
Set in Caledonia

For my little brother now grown big,
William Miller Frank

Contents

Rip~Roaring
RUSSELL

Lost and Found

In September of the year that he was four, going on five, Russell Michaels began going to the Sunshine Nursery School. He was not sure that he wanted to go. Of course, he had heard all about school from the other children who lived in his apartment building and were older than he was. There was Nora Resnick, who was seven years old, and her little brother Teddy, who was five. And there was also Eugene Spencer Eastman, who was eight years old. These friends often played with Russell, and sometimes they even played school. Nora and Eugene Spencer took turns being the teacher and telling the others what to do.

Playing with his friends was always fun for Russell. But attending a real school was not quite the same. True, knowing that he was big enough to go off to school every morning just like the others made him feel grown up. Still, many mornings as his mother helped him get dressed, Russell wished that he could stay home with her the way he did when he was little.

He looked at his baby sister Elisa. She was only a few months old, so she didn't have to go anywhere. How lucky she was to stay home alone in the house with Mommy and do whatever she wanted. She didn't have to listen to the teacher and remember all the nursery school rules like clean-up time and no-push-ing-on-line.

"Russell, you're a big boy now," his mother reminded him when he said that maybe he would stay home too. "Only babies stay in the house with their mommies all day long."

One of the problems with going to school was that Russell always seemed to be losing things. On the very first day of school, he had taken his favorite little car with him.

"I think you should leave that at home," said Mommy.

"No," Russell had insisted. "I'll keep it in my pocket where it will be safe." He felt better knowing that he had his car with him. If he got lonely or sad during the morning, he could take it out of his pocket and play with it. He ran the wheels of the little car along his arm.

"It might get lost," his mother said.

"I'll be careful," Russell told her.

Somehow, during the morning, the car did get lost. Russell didn't even notice it was missing until he came home and was eating his lunch. At first he was very upset, but his mother said that perhaps he would find it the next day. So the following morning Russell returned to school hoping to find the little car. He looked for it in every box of toys and in each corner of the room, but he could not find it. It was lost.

The second week of school, Russell had worn a red baseball cap that his grandfather had sent him in the mail. He was very proud of it. Eugene Spencer had a baseball cap that was blue, but Russell liked red even better. He wanted to wear his hat in class, but Mrs. Lane, who was the teacher, said that a gentleman never wore a hat indoors.

"I'm not a gentleman," said Russell. "I'm a boy."

But Mrs. Lane had insisted, so Russell put his cap in the cubby in his classroom. Later in the morning, when the children went to the little play area on the building's roof, Russell proudly put on his baseball cap again.

Up on the roof there were swings and a slide and even a sandbox. The playground was just like the one in the park except it was high above the street. There was a tall fence all around the roof so that even if the children ran and jumped about, they were in no danger of falling. Russell liked to swing high and look at the rooftops nearby. It was much more fun than swinging in the park, which he had been doing since he was a very little boy. Suddenly, as Russell was swinging, a gust of wind blew his red baseball cap off his head. The wind carried the cap through the air, and there was no way to chase it.

"Look! Look!" the children shouted to one another. They thought a hat flying in the air just like a red bird was funny. Russell didn't think it was funny at all. Losing his baseball cap made him cry.

When his mother came to pick him up, Russell told her what had happened. "Let's look while we're walking home," she said. "Perhaps it landed in the street and we'll find it." But although they walked home very slowly, looking all over the sidewalk and at each curb as they crossed the street, they could not find Russell's cap that had blown away. It was really lost.

One day in October, Russell lost his temper. He punched a boy who kept coming too close to him while he was building in the block corner. "Go away," shouted Russell. He was afraid the boy would knock down his building.

Mrs. Lane saw him. "We don't hit people in this class," she said. She made Russell put all the blocks away and sit by himself for a few minutes. Russell was very angry.

The next day, when Mrs. Lane was busy on the other side of the room, Russell punched the boy again. This time the boy punched back. Russell lost his balance and fell, hitting his mouth against a big pile of blocks. It hurt so much that he started crying and didn't even notice at first what had happened.

Mrs. Lane wiped Russell's face. He thought she was wiping his tears, but then he saw that there was red on the paper towels. He was bleeding.

The sight of the blood was frightening, so Russell cried still harder. Several minutes passed before Mrs. Lane and Russell and the other children realized that Russell had lost his top two teeth.

"I hate that Germy," said Russell to his mother, who came as quickly as she could after Mrs. Lane telephoned her. "I'm never coming back to this school!"

Mrs. Michaels took Russell to the dentist in a taxi. "Germy should go to jail," said Russell, as the car pulled up outside the dentist's office. "Maybe the police will come for him."

"Oh, Russell," said his mother. "Don't be silly. He didn't mean to hurt you. It was an accident. And don't call names," she added.

"He's Germy and I don't like him," said Russell.

The dentist said that there was nothing to do and nothing to worry about. "In two or three years, he'll grow his permanent teeth to

replace the two that he's lost," said the dentist.

"Look," said Russell's mother, relieved that the accident was not more serious. She took a small mirror from her pocketbook and held it so Russell could see his face. "You have a smile just like Nora now." Russell looked in the mirror. He stuck his tongue through the little hole where his top teeth had been earlier in the morning.

He smiled at himself. "I do look like Nora," he said.

"That's right. You have a seven-year-old smile in a four-year-old face," agreed his mother.

Russell went back to school the next day. Everyone wanted to see the space where his teeth used to be. Some of the children had older brothers and sisters who had lost their teeth, but none of them had lost any themselves yet. Russell felt very grown up and special.

Mrs. Lane made Russell share the easel with the boy who had punched him. "I want you two to learn to work and play together," she said.

"Hello, Germy," said Russell. Now that the blood was gone and his lip didn't hurt him, he couldn't even remember why they had been fighting the day before.

"Hi, Russell," said the boy.

They painted a big picture together. When the boy got blue on Russell's side of the paper, Russell didn't even mind. Russell got red paint on the boy's side of the paper, and he didn't mind either. Soon there was red and blue paint all over the paper and some on Russell and the boy too.

When it was time for juice and cookies, they sat together.

"I played with Germy today," Russell reported, when his mother came to pick him up from school.

"That's nice," said his mother. "I'm glad

you boys are friends now. But I wish you wouldn't call him that name." She smiled at her son. "Can't you call him by his real name? That would be a friendlier thing to do."

"He *is* Germy," insisted Russell.

"Germs make people sick," explained Mrs. Michaels. "No one has that for a name." She turned to Mrs. Lane. "What is the name of the boy who pushed Russell yesterday?" she asked.

"There was no pushing today," said Mrs. Lane reassuringly. "They're good friends now."

"Oh, I know," said Mrs. Michaels, "and I'm glad about that. But what's his name?"

"Jeremy," said Mrs. Lane.

"See? I told you," lisped Russell, because he had a little trouble speaking with two of his teeth missing. "His name is Germy."

Mrs. Michaels laughed. "I guess you did," she said. "Perhaps he can come home to lunch with you someday."

"Oh, goody!" shouted Russell.

After that, some days Jeremy came over to play at Russell's house, and some days Russell went to play at Jeremy's house.

"I wish I lost my teeth," said Jeremy, admiring the empty space in Russell's mouth. "Push me hard," he said. "Then I can lose my teeth and look like you. I won't push you back. I promise."

"Pushing isn't nice," Russell reminded Jeremy. So even though from time to time his friend would ask him to, Russell never pushed him again.

In the months that followed, Russell lost his mittens, a scarf, and his temper at the nursery school. But it didn't matter very much. He never found his mittens or his scarf, but he always found his temper again.

One day when Jeremy was playing, he stuck his hand under a radiator in the corner of the classroom. He pulled out a dusty little car that had been hiding there for months.

"It's my car!" shrieked Russell with delight when he saw it. "You found my car!"

Russell was very happy. He had found a new friend in nursery school. And Germy, his friend, had found his old car. Together the two boys built a garage with blocks from the block corner, and they took turns rolling the little car in and out of it. Some days school was lots of fun.

Columbus Day

One morning nursery school was closed. It was Monday, but it was also called Columbus Day and was a holiday. Russell was excited because his mother had told him that there was going to be a big parade and that she would take him to see it. Russell loved parades. He liked to watch the people marching in step and wearing colorful uniforms. He also liked the music. Best of all, he liked the drums.

"Bang. Bang," he shouted, grabbing two blocks and hitting them together when he woke in the morning. He was imagining the parade. If he had a drum, he would ask if he could march in the parade too.

"Russell, hush," said his mother, coming into the bedroom. "Can't you see that Elisa is still sleeping?"

Russell looked across the room to the crib where his little sister slept.

"She was up during the night because she's teething. If we're quiet, she may sleep a little longer," said Mommy.

Russell scowled. His mother was always telling him to quiet down so as not to wake the baby. Yet when Elisa was awake, she made so much noise that he sometimes felt that his parents hardly noticed him, even if he shouted and jumped about. Russell put the blocks down, but he felt angry. The more his mother reminded him to keep quiet these days, the louder he wanted to be.

"It's very cloudy out. I hope it isn't going to rain," his mother said, as Russell started eating his breakfast.

"Won't they have the parade if it rains?" asked Russell.

"I'm pretty sure that they hold it rain or shine," she told him, "but I don't see how we can go if it doesn't clear up. We don't want Elisa to get wet."

"I don't care if she gets wet," said Russell, getting up from the table and stamping his foot. "She gets wet when she has a bath. And she makes her diapers wet all the time."

"That's different," explained his mother. "If she gets wet outdoors, she might get sick."

"I go out in the rain," said Russell. "You made me go to school in the rain last week. You said I wouldn't melt. Elisa won't melt either."

16

"Of course she won't melt," said his mother. "But you are bigger and stronger than she is. Besides, you have your new yellow rain slicker to wear."

"She could wear it," offered Russell, even though he loved his new yellow slicker with its shiny fabric and its hood that protected his head.

They could hear Elisa's cries from the bedroom announcing that she was now awake. "Maybe the sun will come out and we won't have any problems after all," said Mommy hopefully, as she lifted Elisa out of her crib.

Elisa spent the whole morning eating and crying and sleeping and crying some more. Russell spent the whole morning running back and forth to look out the window. Sometimes he thought he saw the sun peeking through the clouds.

He tried building with his Lego pieces but he was too restless. He tried playing with all his little cars, but although some days he could play with them for over an hour, today they weren't any fun. All he could think about was the parade.

Russell heard his mother calling someone on the telephone. "I don't know what to do about the P-A-R-A-D-E," she said. "I don't want to leave E-L-I-S-A with a B-A-B-Y-S-I-T-T-E-R. It's so difficult with her T-E-E-T-H-I-N-G." Russell didn't like it when his mother spoke A-B-C talk. He couldn't understand what she said. "Say words," he always insisted when his parents spoke letters that way.

While he was eating his peanut-butter sandwich for lunch, his mother said, "Russell, I have an idea. I'll phone Mrs. Resnick. She's planning to take Nora and Teddy to the parade. I'm sure you could go with them, and that way I won't have to worry about Elisa getting wet."

"OK," said Russell. He was a little disappointed that his mother wouldn't be coming with him to watch the parade. But the important thing was that he would get to see it regardless of the weather and Elisa. Nora and Teddy were big and didn't have to worry about melting. Babies like Elisa were the ones who could be wet inside the house but not outside.

Russell finished his glass of milk while his mother dialed the phone. He watched her. She held the receiver in her hand a long time, but she didn't say anything.

Finally she put the receiver down. "Russell, there's no answer," she said. "They must have left the house very early."

Russell felt tears in his eyes. But before he had a chance to start crying, his mother dialed the telephone again. "I'm calling Eugene Spencer's number," she explained. Russell thought he would feel very grown up if he went to the parade with such a big boy as Eugene Spencer.

He listened as his mother spoke. "Oh, I see," said Mrs. Michaels. She nodded her head, although of course Eugene Spencer's mother couldn't see her.

"Russell," she said, as she hung up the receiver again, "Eugene Spencer went to the parade with Nora and Teddy."

Russell let out a cry. "You take me. You take me. You promised!" he shouted at his mother.

"I know I promised," she said. "But I didn't think it would rain."

"Take me! Take me!" Russell screamed with anger.

Elisa began crying too. Russell didn't know why she was crying. She didn't even understand about the parade. It was all her fault that they weren't going to see it. Both children howled.

Mrs. Michaels picked up Elisa and rocked her in her arms. "Russell," she said above the noise, "Elisa is getting her teeth. Her gums hurt her. Stop crying and we'll make another plan."

Russell didn't want another plan. He wanted to see the Columbus Day Parade.

Nora and Teddy and Eugene Spencer and all the other children in the city were at the parade, and he had to stay home because he had a baby sister. It wasn't fair at all. He stamped his feet and he howled and howled.

"Come," said his mother, "sit with me on the sofa and we'll talk about it together."

"No," shouted Russell. He ran to his room and grabbed his cars and started to throw them in the air. He hoped they would hit Elisa.

"Stop that," commanded his mother. "I'm going out of this room. When you are calmer, come out and we'll talk together."

There was nothing to talk about, and besides, Russell was crying too hard. He sat down on the floor and kicked his feet against the wooden floor. He threw one of his cars against the wall. He watched as the car landed on the floor. He picked up another one and threw that too. When it landed, the wheels fell off. Now he was angrier than ever. If he hadn't been so angry, he wouldn't have thrown the car. Now the car was broken, and it was all Elisa's fault. He could hear that Elisa was still crying too.

Russell climbed up into his bed and put his pillow over his head so he wouldn't have to listen to that baby crying all the time. The next thing he knew, he was turning over on his bed. He had fallen asleep and taken a nap, just like a baby. He sat up and looked toward the window. Rain was dripping down the pane of glass. Across the room, Elisa was sleeping in her crib. The door to the room was open, and Mommy was standing there. Russell felt like crying again. Not hard, loud cries the way he did in his terrible rage. Now he felt like crying softly, in disappointment. He had wanted to go to the parade so much. His mother came and sat down on the bed beside him. "Poor Russell," she said. "I know you're sad. I'm sad too. I wanted to take you to the parade, just like last year."

"It's all Elisa's fault," sobbed Russell. "Why do we need her?"

"Russell, you can't remember, but not so long ago, you were just as tiny and helpless as she is now. Soon she'll be bigger and you'll have good times playing with her. She will always be your friend, the way Nora and Teddy are friends and play together."

"I don't need her," said Russell. "Eugene Spencer doesn't have any sisters or brothers. He's lucky. He went to the parade, and he doesn't have to share his mommy and daddy with anyone."

Mrs. Michaels reached for a tissue and gave it to Russell. "Mommies and daddies have enough love for all their children. Having a sister doesn't mean that you get less. It isn't like sharing cookies. Love grows bigger and bigger when there are more children in a family. Only cookies and candy grow smaller when there are more people to share them with."

Russell curled up against his mother. He felt good sitting next to her and not having Elisa around. "I wish I saw the parade," he said.

"I know," said his mother. "But next month is November and then we'll go to the Thanksgiving Parade. That parade is even bigger, and there are big balloons and floats."

"Suppose it rains?" Russell said, sniffing.

"On Thanksgiving Day, Daddy won't have to go to work. So he will be able to take you to the parade, and you can go even if it rains," promised Mrs. Michaels.

"Come into the kitchen and I'll give you some milk and cookies," she offered.

Russell got off his bed. He looked on the floor but the little car with the broken wheels was not there. He thought it might have rolled under his bed.

He ate his cookies and talked with his mother. He didn't make any noise, but not because Elisa was napping. He was quiet because he felt quiet inside himself now. Afterwards, he worked on a jigsaw puzzle and finished it all by himself. He was still disappointed about not going to the parade, but he thought about the Thanksgiving Parade. That would be fun.

Elisa woke from her nap and crawled about on the floor. Poor baby, thought Russell. She can't even walk. He was glad that he was a big boy and not bald like Elisa.

When Mr. Michaels came home from work, he reached into his wet coat and took something from the pocket for Russell. It was a little box with a car inside, just like the one that had broken.

"Daddy," said Russell, "take good care of your raincoat."

"Why?" asked Mr. Michaels.

"You may need it on Thanksgiving," Russell explained. "Mommy says we can go to the parade even if it rains."

"Of course," said his father. "We won't melt." He reached into his other pocket and took out a second little box. In it was another car, a new one that Russell didn't have in his collection.

"I'm going to make a parade of all my cars!" shouted Russell, and he ran to his room.

"Ruuuuuummmmmmmm," he shouted. The noise was a happy one, and for once, no one told him to quiet down.

Chinese Dinner

Although his friends' parents were away for the day, Russell was spending Sunday afternoon playing with Nora and Teddy in their apartment. He liked their grandmother and grandfather, who were taking care of them.

Nora knew a lot of riddles, and she was trying to see if her grandparents could guess the answers.

"What's white, has four wheels, and flies?" she asked.

"An airplane!" said her grandfather.

"No. It's a garbage truck!" shouted Teddy. Nora had told him that riddle before.

"Here's another," said Nora. "What's the best way to keep a skunk from smelling?"

"I don't know. There aren't any skunks in the city," said Grandpa.

"Hold his nose!" said Nora, laughing.

"Here's a riddle for you," said Grandpa. "How can we all eat dinner without Grandma having to do any cooking?"

"How?" asked all the children.

"We can go to the Chinese restaurant," said Grandpa.

Everyone cheered. The riddle was a good one, and so was the plan.

"Can Russell come too?" asked Teddy.

"Sure," said Grandpa. "He's getting to be quite a young man. I'd be delighted if he would join us."

Russell smiled. He was glad that he was big

enough to eat dinner with his friends in a real restaurant. Sometimes, on the way home from nursery school, his mother took him to buy pizza. But that wasn't a sit-down restaurant, and besides, Elisa often got restless and started crying. Then Russell would have to finish eating his slice of pizza as they walked home.

While Teddy's Grandma went to telephone Russell's parents to tell them about the dinner plans, Nora thought of a new riddle. "What's big and little at the same time?" she asked.

No one knew the answer.

"Russell," she said. "He's littler than Teddy and me, but bigger than Elisa. He's a big brother."

Russell glowed with delight. He liked being the answer to a riddle, and it was true. He was a big brother. Teddy was only a little brother to Nora. And even Eugene Spencer wasn't a big brother. That was something.

They got their jackets. "Watch me, Teddy's Grandpa," said Russell. He threw his winter jacket on the floor and demonstrated the method he had learned in nursery school for putting it on.

"That looks like fun," said Grandpa, and he threw his coat on the floor too.

"Herman," said Grandma, calling Teddy's Grandpa by his real name. "You'll hurt your back."

"Nonsense," said the old man, putting his arms into his sleeves and flipping his coat on over his head. "This is fun. I think I'll do it this way all the time from now on."

When all the winter coats, scarves, hats and mittens were on, they were ready to leave.

"Have we forgotten anything?" asked Teddy's Grandma.

"Nope," said Grandpa, patting his pocket. "I have the money. There's nothing else we need."

"What about good appetites?" she asked. "Is everyone bringing good appetites along?"

Nora and Teddy laughed. They were used

to their grandparents' jokes. But Russell asked, "What does an appetite look like?"

"It looks like a boy who eats everything on his plate," said Grandma.

"Or a girl," Nora reminded her.

They went downstairs together in the elevator and walked the two blocks to the Chinese restaurant. The wind blew so hard that no one spoke. They just held hands together and kept on walking. Entering the warm restaurant and smelling the food was wonderful.

"A table for five," said Grandpa to the waiter.

"You have a big family," said the waiter, smiling at them all.

"Yes," agreed Grandpa. "Tonight I have a really big family."

They sat down at the table and removed their coats. Then they looked at the big menus that the waiter placed before them.

"I can't read," said Russell.

But Nora and Teddy had eaten in this same restaurant many times before and knew which foods to order without even reading the words at all.

"Won ton soup!" said Teddy.

"Good idea!" said Grandpa. "Let's all have won ton soup."

"It will warm us up," agreed Grandma.

"What's won ton soup?" asked Russell. He was excited about eating in the restaurant with his friends, but he was a little worried too. Perhaps they'd make him eat something that didn't taste good. His mother never cooked won ton soup.

"It's good, Russell. You'll like it," Nora assured him.

The waiter went off and soon returned carrying a tray with five bowls of won ton soup.

"Mmmmmmm," said Grandma. "This looks very good."

"I don't want the leaves in my soup," said Teddy, pointing to the bits of green floating in his bowl. "I never eat them."

"Just leave them there," said his grandmother.

"No," said Teddy. "Mommy always takes them out for me."

"I only want soup. I don't want ravioli," said Russell, pointing to his bowl of soup.

"These aren't ravioli. These are won ton," explained Nora.

"I only want won ton, not soup," she said, looking into her own bowl.

"I like leaves," said Russell, fishing a bit of greenery from his bowl.

"Just a minute," said Grandpa. He took the green leaves out of Teddy's bowl and put them into Russell's bowl. Then he took the won ton out of Russell's bowl and put them into Nora's bowl. He poured some of the broth from Nora's bowl into Teddy's bowl and some into Russell's bowl.

"Can I eat your won ton since you aren't eating them?" asked Nora. Grandpa stopped his maneuvers and looked into his own bowl.

"Sure," he said. He took the won ton out of his bowl and put them into Nora's bowl.

35

"Here's another piece of green that you missed," said Teddy. He removed it with his fingers and put it into Grandpa's bowl.

"This plain soup is good," said Russell.

"Let me taste it," said Grandpa, looking into his own bowl again. "Yes," he agreed, "it's a little cool, but it's good."

"We forgot to put noodles in our soup," said Nora. She reached for the dish of crunchy Chinese noodles and put some into her bowl. Teddy and Russell each took big handfuls of noodles to put into their bowls, and the noodles were all gone.

"We can get more from the waiter," said Grandma, signalling to the man serving food.

The waiter brought a large bowl of noodles. While they were waiting for the other dishes of food, Russell looked around at the diners sitting at nearby tables.

"Look at that man eating with sticks!" he exclaimed with surprise. "What a funny way to eat food!"

"Those are chopsticks," Teddy said.

"We tried eating with them, but it's too hard," said Nora. "Everything falls back into your plate. I only like to use chopsticks when I'm not hungry."

"In China, people use those sticks for eating," Grandpa explained. "They think forks are strange."

When the waiter came with the rest of the food, Grandpa asked him for a pair of chopsticks. Russell looked at them. They were smooth and were thicker than the knitting needles that his mother was using to make a sweater for Elisa. Teddy's Grandpa showed Russell how to use the sticks. But Russell couldn't manage them at all.

"I told you they don't work very good," said Nora, watching him.

"The very best way to eat is with your fingers," said Teddy. He was chewing on a barbecued sparerib.

Russell agreed. He picked up a rib and began to eat it with his fingers too.

"Here's an egg roll," said Teddy's grandmother, putting one on Russell's plate.

"I don't see any egg inside here," said Russell, examining the item on his plate.

The waiter had brought other things too. There was sweet and sour chicken and beef with broccoli.

"You know I don't like broccoli," said Teddy, passing up that dish. But he ate all the pieces of pineapple that were mixed in with the chicken.

Nora ate an egg roll and some fried rice.

Russell took a tiny bit of everything and decided that the egg rolls were best. So he ate a whole egg roll and left the other things on his plate for a while. Then he nibbled on the beef and broccoli and the fried rice.

Grandma and Grandpa scraped out the dishes and ate whatever the children passed up. "This sweet and sour chicken is very good," said Grandma.

Dessert was easy to order. The choice was vanilla or chocolate ice cream. The three children chose chocolate and the adults chose vanilla.

"I don't want to be a grown-up," said Russell.

"Why not?" asked Grandpa.

"Grown-ups eat vanilla. I like chocolate," said Russell.

"Some grown-ups eat chocolate," said Nora. "Look over there." She pointed to a man at the next table who was eating chocolate ice cream.

"Nora, it's not polite to point," corrected Grandma.

A dish of fortune cookies came with the ice cream. There was a cookie for each person. Everyone took one and broke it in half to discover the message inside. Grandpa read them all aloud.

Nora's said: "Life is a riddle and few learn its answer."

Teddy's said: "You have both the desire and the ability to express your many talents."

Russell's said: "Be careful not to forget anything."

Grandma's said: "Focus your attention on business and professional matters."

Grandpa's said: "You have the ability to smooth over problems and make people happy."

"You make me happy," said Nora.

"Me too," said Teddy and Russell and Grandma.

"Good," said Grandpa, crunching down on a bite of his fortune cookie. "Then I'm glad that we all came here for dinner."

"Can we come again?" asked Russell.

"Some day, but not too soon," replied Grandpa.

"Why not?" asked Nora. "It's fun."

"It wouldn't be such a special treat if we came all the time," he explained. "Besides, it's hard work for me when we come here, fixing up the soups and everything."

Russell nodded his head understandingly.

"Time to go," said Grandma, standing up. "Don't forget anything."

They all put on their coats, scarves, hats and mittens. Russell didn't notice that he had forgotten his mittens until they were all outside in the cold air.

"We should have known he would," said Nora. "That was his fortune."

So they all went back inside the restaurant and found the mittens waiting under the chair where he had put them for safekeeping.

BE CAREFUL NOT TO FORGET ANYTHING

Why Russell Was Late

One Monday morning in early spring, Russell woke up and decided he didn't want to go to school. He remembered that Jeremy had been absent all the week before.

"I want to stay home," he whined when his mother started to help him dress for school.

"Don't be silly," said Mrs. Michaels. "Of course you want to go to school."

"No, I don't," said Russell. He wasn't sure
why. He just wanted to stay home the way he
had when he was little, before Elisa was born.

"Aren't you feeling well?" asked his mother.
She felt his forehead. "Let me see your
tongue."

Russell stuck out his tongue for his mother
to see.

"Your head is cool, and your tongue is very
red. You're in fine shape," his mother diag-
nosed. "I don't care," insisted Russell. "I want
to stay home."

"But you like your school," his mother reminded him. "You have a good time there and
nice friends to play with."

"Germy was absent," said Russell.

"Jeremy got chicken pox last week," Mrs.
Michaels said. "You've already had chicken
pox. And besides, Jeremy will be back in
school before long and looking for you."

"Elisa stays home, and she isn't sick,"
whined Russell. "I want to stay home too."

Mrs. Michaels laughed. "Elisa is a baby.

You're not. You've just had your fifth birthday. You are a very big boy now."

Russell didn't think it was fair at all. He wished that he were the baby and that Elisa went to school. Then he could stay home and have lots of fun. Russell started to cry.

"I don't want to go to school," he howled.

"It's OK if he stays home one day," said Mr. Michaels, buttoning his coat and going towards the door.

"What about T-O-M-O-R-R-O-W?" asked Mrs. Michaels. "He'll always want to S-T-A-Y H-O-M-E."

"I doubt it," said Mr. Michaels, as the door closed behind him.

Russell sat down on the floor and cried as hard as he could. Just then Elisa began to cry too. Her crying was always very loud and, as usual, it sent their mother running.

Russell shouted above the baby's cries. "I want to stay home and be your baby the way I used to be before Elisa was born." He began to pull off his clothing and to kick on the floor with both feet. He didn't want to be a big boy.

At first his mother ignored him, so he just cried louder and harder. "I want to stay home," he yelled over and over again.

At last his mother gave in. "All right," she shouted above Elisa's screams. "Stay home and be a baby. See if I care."

Russell stopped crying immediately. He went into the kitchen to celebrate his triumph with breakfast. He knew he was going to have a good time at home. While he was still deciding between crispy Frosty Bits or crunchy Tasty Pops, his mother came into the kitchen. She put Elisa into her high chair. Then she placed a steaming bowl in front of Russell.

"Yuck!" said Russell, and he made a face. "What is this?"

"It's nutritious rice cereal. Elisa eats it every morning unless she has hot oatmeal instead."

"I don't want any," said Russell, pushing the bowl away.

"Oh, but you must," his mother insisted. And she put a spoonful of the white glop into his mouth before he had time to shut it. That was the way she fed Elisa. The cereal was awful. Russell wanted to spit it out, but he remembered that whenever Elisa did that, his mother managed to shovel the food right back inside her mouth again. So he held his mouth firmly closed and swallowed instead.

"Every little baby starts off the day with hot cereal," his mother said.

Elisa was no longer crying now that she had her cereal. Russell watched her eating it. She actually seemed to like it. He wondered if the cereal would taste better with some sugar, but he was afraid to open his mouth and suggest it. He didn't want his mother to put another hot, sticky spoonful into his mouth.

While his mother washed off Elisa's face, Russell ran into the living room to turn on the television. It would be fun to see which programs were shown on Monday morning.

"Oh, no!" his mother said, running after him and shutting off the set. "Babies don't watch television. If you want to be a baby, then you'll have to amuse yourself with some toys." Russell was annoyed that his mother wouldn't let him watch TV, but it was still more fun to stay home and be a baby than to go off to school. So he went to his room to find something to play with. He took his box of Lego off the shelf and started to build with it.

"You naughty child," Mrs. Michaels called out. "You can't play with such tiny pieces. You might swallow them."

"I don't put toys in my mouth," Russell protested. "I always play with my Lego."

"Not when you're a baby," said his mother. "Today you are my other baby. Come with me. This is how we keep babies out of mischief." She led Russell to Elisa's playpen and helped him climb inside.

"Now you stay there and play," she said.

Elisa sat in one corner of the playpen and

stared at her brother. She seemed to think his being there was a big joke. At first Russell thought it was funny too. He pretended that the two of them were lions at the zoo. He made loud, growling sounds as if he were a lion. Then he pretended that they were astronauts inside a space capsule. But the playpen was small and cramped, and Elisa didn't really know how to play at all. She chewed happily on a rubber dog, and from time to time, she rattled some plastic discs that were attached by a chain.

After a short while, Russell grew bored. It seemed time to make a getaway, so he climbed out of the playpen and went looking for his mother.

She was vacuuming in the next room.

"I'm hungry," Russell complained over the noise of the vacuum cleaner. He had eaten only one spoonful of cereal at breakfast.

His mother didn't say a word. She turned off the machine and went into the kitchen. When

she returned, she was holding a baby bottle
filled with warm milk. "This is the mid-morn-
ing snack that Elisa gets every day."

Russell took the bottle. He thought it would
be fun to drink from it the way Elisa did. But
only a tiny squirt of the milk came out of the
nipple, and the taste of warm milk wasn't very
good.

"Yuck!" he said.

"Warm milk is cocoa without the chocolate
flavoring," said his mother. "It will make you
grow."

"Give me cocoa instead," said Russell,
handing her the bottle.

"Babies don't get chocolate," she replied.
"Come, it's time for your nap."

"What nap?" asked Russell. "I don't need a
nap. I slept all night long."

"All growing babies must have a morning
nap," his mother reminded him. "You always
had a nap when you were a little baby."

Russell couldn't remember. It was too long

ago. "What happens after nap time?" he asked.

"Lunch. Delicious mashed carrots and mashed peas. And for dessert there is mashed banana. That's Elisa's favorite. It was your favorite when you were a baby too."

"Yuck!" said Russell, making a face. "That stuff sounds awful."

"After lunch you can play in the playpen some more," said his mother, smiling.

Elisa began to cry in the playpen. Poor thing, thought Russell. She has to stay inside there every day. Mrs. Michaels went to pick her up. "Isn't it nice that I have two babies," she said. "You can both take your naps at the same time."

"YUCK!" Russell yelled. "I don't want to be a baby anymore. I forgot how yucky it is."

His mother started laughing. "Oh, Russell," she said, bending down to give him a hug, with Elisa still in her arms. "Being a baby when you're very little is wonderful. It's just not so much fun when you're big."

"Is it too late to go to school?" asked Russell.

"I don't know what time it is," said his mother.

Russell ran into the kitchen to look at the clock. "The big foot is on the six, and the little foot is on the ten," he reported.

"Foot?" asked his mother. "Oh, you mean hand," she corrected him.

What she said didn't make sense to Russell. Those things on the clock didn't look like either hands or feet, really. But as it was only 10:30 in the morning, his mother told him to get his sneakers, which were under his bed. Meanwhile, Mrs. Michaels dressed Elisa and got her ready to go outside.

"The baby can sleep in the carriage," Mrs. Michaels said. Together they pushed the carriage. Elisa put her thumb in her mouth. Her eyes began to close, then to open, and then to close again. She was taking her morning nap.

As they walked, Russell ate a snack his mother gave him to keep him going, since he had had such a small breakfast. He had two oatmeal cookies and a little box of raisins. Nothing mashed.

When he got to school, everyone in the class wanted to know why Russell was so late.

"It's a secret," he said.

Staying Up Late

When his mother and Elisa came to pick him up at nursery school one day, Russell had exciting news. "Guess what's going to be on TV tonight?" he said.

"I've no idea," answered Mrs. Michaels. "What?"

"*Chitty Chitty Bang Bang*. It's all about a car that can fly."

"That doesn't sound possible," said Russell's mother. "Do you know what time it's on? Don't forget tomorrow is a school day and you need your sleep."

"I don't know," said Russell, "but everyone in my class is going to watch it. We all talked about it."

When they got back to the apartment, Mrs. Michaels checked the television schedule in the newspaper.

"Russell," she called out, "that movie doesn't even begin until 8 P.M. It's much too late for you to watch. It won't be over for hours. A little boy like you needs his sleep."

"I'm not little," said Russell, stamping his foot. "I'm big! When I want to stay home from school, you say that I'm a big boy and I have to go. When I climbed into Elisa's crib, you said I was a big boy and I would break it."

"You'll see it another time," said Mrs. Michaels.

"No," said Russell. "Everyone in my class will see it except me. Germy's going to watch it on TV. He told me he would."

"I don't care what Jeremy is going to do. You need your sleep," said Mrs. Michaels. "And that's final."

"It's not fair," said Russell, trying hard not to cry. If he cried he would seem like a baby, and he wanted to impress his mother with the fact that he was quite grown up. "Sometimes you say I'm little, and sometimes you say I'm big. I feel big enough to stay up and watch TV."

"You're not a baby," agreed his mother. "But you're not a grown-up either. Only grown-ups can stay awake so late at night."

Russell thought for a minute. "I know what," he said. "I could take a nap the way Elisa does. Then would you let me stay up late?"

"I'm taking you to get your hair cut this afternoon," Mrs. Michaels reminded him. "Your hair is so long you can hardly see. When would there be time for you to take a nap?"

"I could go to sleep right after supper the

way Elisa does, and then you could wake me up in time to see the program," suggested Russell. He was proud of his idea. It seemed like a good one to him.

"Would you really go to sleep and not fool around in bed?" asked his mother. "No playing with cars under the blankets or anything like that?

"Let me see," she said. "If you fell asleep by 6:30 and I woke you at 8, then you would make up an hour and a half of the sleep you would be missing."

"Goody!" shouted Russell. "I can do it. Rummmmmm," he yelled with delight, running about the apartment. It was the first time he had convinced Mommy to change her mind by talking with her. Usually he had a tantrum and cried and kicked the floor. Sometimes a tantrum worked and sometimes it didn't. Mommy always said that big boys talked and didn't yell and scream. Russell decided that the method really worked.

That afternoon, Elisa stayed home with a

baby-sitter, and Russell went with his mother to get his hair cut. He came home with one lollipop in his pocket and one in his mouth. His hair had been cut and plastered down with a liquid that the barber had put on his head, and Russell felt that he looked very grown up.

Mr. Michaels had a business meeting and wasn't home for supper. Russell's mother served the food earlier than usual. He had a lamb chop, a baked potato, and peas. Elisa had the same things but they were all mushed up and cut into tiny pieces. For dessert Russell had his second lollipop. Then he took his bath, washing himself while his mother gave Elisa her bedtime bottle. The clock said only twenty minutes past six when he was ready for bed.

"Good," said his mother. "Perhaps you will get an extra few minutes of sleep if you hurry."

Mommies always worried about sleep and food, thought Russell as he climbed into his bed. "Good night," said Mommy, tucking him into bed.

"Good night," said Russell.

"Good night, Elisa," said Mommy. "Don't keep your big brother awake. He needs his sleep."

Russell laughed. It was a good joke to think that Elisa might keep him awake. Usually his mother scolded because he was going to wake her.

Their mother turned off the light and closed the door. Elisa didn't seem to notice. She kept on jabbering in her baby talk. Russell listened and wondered if she thought she was saying real words to him. After a while, Elisa stopped talking and put her thumb in her mouth. Even though the room was dark, Russell knew she had because of the little sucking sounds she made. She always did that just before she fell asleep. Russell turned in his bed. He wasn't sleepy at all. It was too early. He wondered if putting his thumb in his mouth would help him fall asleep. His right thumb fitted into the space where his top two teeth were missing. The thumb had a soapy taste from his bath. It was awful and so he took it out. Perhaps Elisa's thumb tasted better, but his wasn't any good at all.

Suddenly Russell had a terrible thought. Suppose he fell asleep and his mother didn't remember to wake him in time? He jumped out of bed and went to find his mother. She was in the kitchen, talking on the telephone.

"Russell, what are you doing out of bed?" she asked.

"Promise me that you'll really wake me up," demanded Russell.

"Of course I'll wake you up, but only if you go to sleep this minute. Now march right to bed," she said.

"If you don't wake me up, I'll never speak to you again," Russell warned his mother.

"Russell! Enough of this. I'm trying to speak on the phone, and you are supposed to be sleeping."

Russell turned and went back to his bedroom. He decided that his threat had shown his mother how important this TV program was. He got back into bed and thought about tomorrow at school. He wondered if the others in his class would really get to see the program. All the children had said that they would watch, but he knew that other parents could be just as fussy and difficult as his own. Perhaps he would be the only one in nursery school who got to see the movie.

He turned over and cuddled under his blanket. He wished that he could fall asleep so the time would pass quicker. He wished it was time to wake up.

"Wake up," said his mother.

"What?" asked Russell. The light was hurting his eyes.

"Wake up. It's almost time for your movie."

"Turn off the light. My eyes hurt," said Russell, pulling the blanket over his head.

His mother switched off the lamp. "Don't you want to see your program?" she asked. Russell didn't know what she was talking about. It couldn't be time to get up for school. He felt much too tired to go to school anyhow.

"Come on," coaxed his mother. "If you want to see it, you'd better get up."

"Shall I carry you?" asked another voice. His father was speaking. Russell felt himself being lifted up. He closed his eyes and snuggled next to his father's sweater. It felt cozy and warm. Then he felt himself being dropped down. He was on the sofa. Russell opened his eyes for a minute.

"What are you doing?" he asked. "Can't I sleep in my bed tonight?"

His mother turned on the television set. "Here is your program," she said. "I woke you just as I promised."

Russell nodded his head. His eyes closed again. He couldn't make them stay open at all. He vaguely remembered asking his mother to promise something, but he couldn't remember what it was. It couldn't be very important, he decided. He opened his eyes once more, but the lids felt so heavy that they shut again al-

most immediately. In the background, he could hear the music of the television. He thought the sound was nice.

Someone shook him. "Russell, open your eyes if you want to see the movie."

Russell opened his eyes and tried to focus on his mother. "A child needs his sleep," he said and closed his eyes again. In his sleep he could hear his mother laughing.

"You're my witness. I tried to wake him. I really did," she said.

"He'll never believe you in the morning," said his father's voice.

Russell wondered what they were talking about, but he was much too tired to care. He felt a blanket being placed over him. It made him feel cozier than ever. He felt as if he could sleep and sleep.

"Wake up," his mother said, shaking him gently. Russell opened his eyes. He was curled up in a ball on the living-room sofa.

"What happened to my bed?" he asked.

Slowly Russell began to remember. "Why didn't you wake me for the television program? You promised you would. You made me go to bed early especially so I could see it."

"I tried to wake you," said his mother. "I really tried. Daddy carried you out here last night, and we turned on the television set, and the entire program played itself out. I don't think you saw any of it."

"I didn't," said Russell, pouting. "It isn't fair. I wanted to see that movie and instead I went to bed early just like a baby." Tears welled up in Russell's eyes.

"You're not a baby. You're my big boy," said his mother, giving him a hug. "Come, let's get ready for you to go to school."

"I bet everyone else saw the movie," Russell complained as he ate his bowl of cereal.

"Maybe they did and maybe they didn't," said his mother. "Wait and see."

That afternoon when Mrs. Michaels came to pick him up from school, Russell called out, "Guess what?"

"Oh, no. Not another late television program?" asked his mother.

"No," said Russell. "No one in my whole class saw the movie. But Germy's father has a machine that copied the movie and he invited me to come to his house after school on Friday to see it."

"Well, I'm glad there's a happy ending to this episode and that you won't have to stay up so late again," said his mother. "It all has worked out just fine."

"Yes," agreed Russell, smiling happily so that the empty space showed where his teeth were missing.

The Parade

Jeremy had come over to play with Russell. "Hey, I know what," he said. "Let's have a parade. We can march around the house."

"Two people can't be a parade," said Russell. "You need lots of people." He thought for a minute. "Maybe Nora and Teddy are home. They could play with us."

He ran to ask his mother to help him dial the telephone. "We want to have a parade," he explained.

"Parades are too noisy for inside the house," said Mrs. Michaels.

Russell was about to argue, when his mother added, "They're wonderful for outdoors. Let's see if Teddy and Nora can meet you outside. You can have your parade up the street. Then you can make all the noise you want, and you'll have more space too."

That was a good idea.

"I'll ask Eugene Spencer to come too," said Russell.

After his calls were completed, he began to look around the house for things that would be useful in a parade. He wished that he hadn't lost his red baseball cap, but he had an old hat of his father's that he used when he played. He would take that.

"Here, Germy," he said. "You can use this." It was a horn that he had gotten at a birthday party a few weeks ago.

For himself, Russell had a whistle on a string that he used when playing with his cars. He would blow on that. When they were all equipped, they went to the elevator. Mrs. Michaels came too, pushing Elisa in her stroller. "Can Elisa be in the parade too?" she asked.

"No," said Russell. "This isn't a parade for babies. Only big children can be in a parade."

Outside the building they found Nora and Teddy and Nora's classmate Sharon waiting for them. They were holding two American flags and talking to their neighbor, old Mrs. Wurmbrand. Mrs. Wurmbrand was the oldest person who lived in Russell's apartment building. She was very fond of Russell's sister Elisa, who was the youngest person in the building. However, she loved all the children in the house and was considered to be an extra grandmother to them all.

Today as she greeted everyone, she was sitting in a wheelchair.

"She fell and broke her hip," Russell explained to Jeremy. "Now she has to be in a wheelchair and someone has to push her, just the way my mother pushes Elisa."

"How are you feeling?" Mrs. Michaels asked the elderly woman.

Mrs. Wurmbrand smiled. "I can't go dancing. But otherwise I'm doing fine," she said.

"Russell, let me see how big you've grown," said Mrs. Wurmbrand.

Russell came next to the wheelchair and stood up very straight and tall.

"Elisa is lucky to have such a big brother," said their old friend. "I always wanted to have a big brother when I was a little girl." Then she looked at Nora and Teddy. "I wanted a little brother too," she said. "I was an only child. It's much better to have more than one child in a family."

All the children smiled at the old woman. It was hard to imagine that someone with so much white hair and so many wrinkles in her face had ever been a child at all.

"What are you going to do now?" asked

Mrs. Wurmbrand. "Are you going to the park?"

"We're going to have a parade. It's going to be right here on the street. You can watch us," suggested Russell.

Just then Eugene Spencer came out of the building. He was carrying a drum and drumsticks. "Can I lead the parade?" he asked.

"No," said Russell. "It's my parade. So I'm going to be first."

"Well, I'm older than you," said Eugene Spencer. "I think I should be first."

"It was my idea," remembered Jeremy.

"It's our street," said Teddy.

"Ladies first," said Nora.

"You're not a lady," shouted Russell. "You're only a little girl."

"I'm not little. I'm bigger than you," Nora reminded him.

"The wonderful thing about a parade," said Mrs. Wurmbrand, "is that every part of it is equally important. People just keep watching.

They want to see everything. I never remember what was first and what was second. I just remember the whole thing together."

Russell thought of the parade his father had taken him to see on Thanksgiving Day, and he nodded his head in agreement. The drums were important. The baton twirlers were important. The floats were important. The horses were important.

Mrs. Wurmbrand's daughter, who was Miss Wurmbrand, came out of the building. She was holding a scarf that she had gone to get for her mother. "I don't want you catching a chill," she said, as she wrapped it around the old lady's neck.

"We're going to have a parade, and you can watch us," said Russell.

"That's fine with me," said Miss Wurmbrand. "It gets a little boring just standing here. I'm glad for a diversion."

"Russell," said old Mrs. Wurmbrand. "I have a very special favor to ask you."

Russell looked at his friend in the wheelchair. He couldn't imagine what she would ask him.

"I've seen many parades in my life. After all, I'm past eighty-six years old, so I've had time to go to many, many parades. But do you know, I've never, ever had a chance to be inside a parade. Could I be in your parade too?"

"But you can't march," said Russell. "You have to stay in your chair."

"I could push her," offered Eugene Spencer. "I'm very strong," he said, making a fist and showing off the muscle in his arm.

"Then I could use your drum," said Russell. "That's a good idea."

The children began to assemble for the parade. First was Russell, holding Eugene Spencer's drum. Behind him was Jeremy. He held Russell's horn. Next were Nora and her friend Sharon, each holding a flag. "We're going to march in step together," she explained to the others. Behind them was Teddy.

Russell had given him the whistle, since he would be busy with the drum. Last of all came Eugene Spencer, pushing Mrs. Wurmbrand in the wheelchair.

"All right. Ready, get set, go," shouted Russell, and he began to beat on the drum and take a few, slow steps toward the corner of the block. Mrs. Michaels stood on the stoop, holding onto the stroller. "Good-bye," she waved. "You can march all around the block, but don't cross any streets."

Elisa started to howl.

"Stop the parade," shouted Nora.

Everyone stopped.

"What's the matter?" asked Russell.

"I think Elisa should be in this parade too."

"She's a baby," said Eugene Spencer, from the end of the line. "She can't walk. How can she be in the parade?"

"I can't walk, and I'm in the parade," Mrs. Wurmbrand reminded them all.

"I'll push her," said Nora, rushing toward the stroller.

"No, you won't," said Russell. "She's my sister. I'll push her."

"Then who gets the drum?" asked Teddy.

"I want the drum!" said Jeremy. "I thought up the parade."

"This is my street," said Teddy.

"I want the drum," said Nora. "I'm older than you."

"I want the drum," said Mrs. Wurmbrand. "I'm older than all of you added together. Besides, I've never beat on a drum before."

Russell gave the drum to Mrs. Wurmbrand. "Hit it loud and hard," he instructed her.

"Of course," said the old woman. "That's the way they always beat the drums in a parade."

So they lined up again. Elisa was in the very front, and Russell was behind her, holding onto the handlebar of the stroller.

"Be very careful," shouted Mrs. Michaels. "Elisa has never been in a parade before."

"Don't worry," called Mrs. Wurmbrand. "Everything will be fine."

Then off they went. Elisa, Russell, Jeremy, Nora and Sharon, Teddy, and Mrs. Wurmbrand, pushed by Eugene Spencer. It wasn't a very large parade, nor was it as colorful or as noisy as most of the ones usually held in the city. But as there were no other parades around that Saturday afternoon in April, everyone on the street stopped to watch. They went first to the corner and then made a left turn. They marched down the next street and made another turn. In all, they turned four times and ended up right where they had started, without having to cross any streets.

Along the way they passed several acquaintances from the neighborhood, who waved to them.

One of the people they met was Mrs. Ellsworth. She was coming out of the bank on the corner. Mrs. Ellsworth was a worrier and a complainer. She always stopped to comment to Russell's mother that the weather was too hot or too cold or looked like rain. She worried if she heard Russell sneeze or if she saw Elisa

chewing on the strap that held her in her carriage. "Germs are everywhere!" she would say with a sigh.

Now for once, Mrs. Ellsworth stood speechless. Then she found something to say. "Mrs. Wurmbrand," she called. "You are too old for playing games with these children. Especially in your present condition."

Nora tapped Jeremy's shoulder, "We call her Mrs. Mind-Your-Own-Business," she explained. "But she never does."

"Come and join us, if you want," said Mrs. Wurmbrand, and she banged on the drum harder than ever.

Mrs. Ellsworth looked a little doubtful. "I'll look silly," she said.

"No, you won't, " said Russell. And so there was a new addition to the marchers.

When they returned to Russell's building, they were all laughing.

"How was the parade?" asked Mrs. Michaels.

"It was splendid," said Mrs. Wurmbrand. "I've seen more parades than anyone here, so I know. It was one of the very best parades ever."

She beat on the drum for attention. "And now, I think all the marchers and all the riders should advance to the corner one more time. I'm going to buy everyone an ice cream cone to celebrate my participation in this grand event."

"Then we better leave the drum and the horns and the flags here," said Russell. "It will be hard to march and hold them and eat ice cream at the same time."

"Good thinking," said Mrs. Wurmbrand.

So they rested all their things together in a pile, and Mrs. Michaels and Miss Wurmbrand promised to watch them. Then off they marched once more. No drums or horns made any noise this time, but Russell shouted and cheered all the way.

He was joined by Elisa. Even though she

had celebrated her first birthday a few weeks ago, she still couldn't talk. But she knew how to make happy noises too. "Ruuuuuu-mmmmmmm," she shouted, as the parade marched off to buy the ice cream.

Mrs. Wurmbrand was right, thought Russell. It was good not to be an only child. Two together could make much more noise.

ABOUT THE AUTHOR

Johanna Hurwitz was born in New York City. She attended Queens College and has a degree in library science from Columbia University. She has been a children's librarian with the New York Public Library and has worked in a variety of library positions in New York and Long Island as well as teaching college courses in children's literature. Mrs. Hurwitz is the author of several popular books about Russell's neighbors, *Busybody Nora* and *Superduper Teddy*. She and her family now live in Great Neck, New York.

ABOUT THE ILLUSTRATOR

Lillian Hoban was born and raised in Philadelphia where she studied at the School of Industrial Art. She has been a children's book author and illustrator for over twenty years and is the creator of many books that have become children's favorites, among them the beloved books about Frances the badger and Arthur the chimpanzee. She is also the illustrator of the popular series by Miriam Cohen about Jim and his first-grade class. Lillian Hoban lives in Connecticut and New York City.